Ben's Flight South

Ben Willis

Illustrator- Mary-Ann Holland

AuthorHouse™
1663 Liberty Drive
Bloomington, IN 47403
www.authorhouse.com
Phone: 1-800-839-8640

First published by AuthorHouse   10/29/2010

ISBN: 978-1-4520-4633-4 (sc)

Library of Congress Control Number: 2010909662

Printed in the United States of America
Bloomington, Indiana

This book is printed on acid-free paper.

authorHOUSE®

Dec. 2010

Gift

I would like to dedicate this book to my parents Kerry and Kim Willis along with my grandparents Irvin and Helen Millis and Clement and Norma Willis. I would like to thank them for starting me off at a young age of learning how to appreciate nature and to always put back what I take out. Without my parents encouragement I would never have been able to complete this book and get it published. Thank you all and I love yall very much.

A cool crisp breeze filled the air with the sound of rustling leaves. The change in colors in the leaves which a few weeks ago were just beginning, now were very easy to discern. Irvin a Canadian goose and Ben his grandson were preparing to set out on a search mission from Canada to find a place for a wintering ground for the rest of their gaggle of geese. Irvin being the older goose, had been on many search missions before and on a few occasions taken his grandson. This search mission was going to be different than previous ones. Irvin told Ben that they would separate and then meet at a location in the Eastern Flyway. The geese often migrated to in Eastern North Carolina.

Irvin told Ben that many things had changed since he last flew in the area. Ben said he would be alert to the changes and knew what to expect because not that much could have changed in five years. The rest of the gaggle was depending on them to find a safe place with food available and clean water.

One morning the frost fell on the ground and covered the ground with a white thick blanket of ice, Irvin signaled to Ben that it was time to begin their mission. The mission began later that morning with Ben and Irvin heading south from Canada to locate a place for the rest of the geese to meet up with them in the later months. Irvin told Ben to fly down the western part of the flyway and he would go down the coastline. They agreed to meet again in eastern North Carolina. Taking wing and flying strong with the North wind at their backs, they reached the border of Canada and the USA by lunch time that day and decided to take a break in the Great Lakes before they set off on the long flight to North Carolina. After eating some mussels and grass on the edge of the lake, Irvin started telling Ben about a few of the changes and the new things that had started happening in the Eastern Flyway.

Ben although younger and less experienced felt he knew more about the ways of the world than his granddad so he just pretended to pay attention. Ben did not know that Irvin was warning him of what to expect along the flight that might put him in danger. The next morning with the sun just peaking above the horizon and the wind nearly calm, the two geese got an early start for their flight. After a quick breakfast in a corn field that used to hold marsh grass,

Irvin made his way toward the East Coast of Delaware and down the waterway of the eastern shore of Maryland by night. Meanwhile, Ben flew straight south winding along the Mississippi river as it too made its way south. He struggled to find areas and fields that he remembered held food and water. He noticed that many of them had been replaced with lots of hard black lots filled with the human's cars and buildings that used to hold fields and river edges. Eventually, he turned and began to fly over Tennessee into North Carolina.

Most of the western area of North Carolina still appeared familiar with its forests and lakes where it seemed to not hold large amounts of the development he had seen up North. He stopped by a sign for the boating ramp of the National Forest at the lake where he paused to rest and eat.   Both geese made great time reaching their destination in eastern North Carolina in three days.

Ben arrived just a few hours before Irvin. When Irvin arrived, Ben seemed to be in shock because of all the changes he noticed along his way down south. He began telling Irvin of all the things that had changed along the flyway. He told Irvin about the cars and parking lots replacing the food places and how the water was dirty and smelled strong in many of the streams that only a few years ago had been clear and filled with trout and mussels and grass to eat. Irvin listened as Ben told him about having a hard time finding places to stop and rest because the fields and ponds he once knew were all gone and replaced by big hard structures.

Irvin took time to explain to Ben all the things that he had seen on his flight down. Ben knew what a road was and what cars and trucks were. He did not know that roads could be so big until he saw some of the interstates that had been developed. In the areas he remembered as forests, ponds, and streams with clean water, he found buildings and more dirty water and smelly air around those areas. Irvin told Ben that these big roads allowed people to travel but not always faster because at times the roads became congested and the air turned nasty around those areas with car fumes. The humans plan for what is best for them but they cause many problems in nature with their actions.

He told Ben how the roads create runoff of mud and silt into into the streams and the rivers that feed into ponds and lakes. He related that the dirty water that flowed from the buildings with smokestacks carried many bad things in the water that kill the plants and animals in the streams. "Ben," he said, "Runoff is a terrible thing. It creates a lot of problems for us and man." He continued to explain how runoff contaminates the water, kills fish and could cause algae blooms that smothered all the oxygen needed by the fish to breathe. "Algae sucks up the oxygen in the water and this kills all the creatures that live in the water and the lack of sunlight kills the good grasses that supply food to the fish as well", Irvin said.

Irvin said that this dirty water seeps into ground and eventually into the water that the humans drink. "When this happens and the people drink the water, Ben it causes many problems for the humans including sickness and even at times death". Ben shook his head in amazement at the things that humans do to the environment.

Home Sweet Home

"What are the hard structures?" Ben asked. Irvin began to explain the big hard structures that Ben had seen which had replaced many of the fields he had once known and where he used to stop in to rest and eat. "The structures that you saw are called malls, high rise buildings and housing complexes and factories. A mall is a place that houses many stores in one location and is where people go to buy things for other people. Humans think a mall makes their lives easier because they go to one place and can get everything they need. A high rise building is usually a group of offices where humans work. They often feel that a large building makes their company more prestigious and makes them more important. The housing complexes are homes, often the extremely large ones are called mansions. People allow themselves to feel the need to live in a big house and often forget about the environment.

The problem with these types of structures is that they create the same runoff problems as the highways. The humans cut down the trees and the marsh grasses that hold the runoff and plant short grass and drain the wet areas that we geese use to eat and rest in on the trip south. They take up places that were once farms or wooded areas that helped keep the environment clean."

Who is going to be responsible?

Ben asked Irvin, "Why do people keep building these things even if they know that it will hurt the environment in some way?" Irvin told Ben he does not know the answer to that question. He says, "Humans are very unusual. They think that someone else should take care of the environment. Humans have a tendency to value what they want, but want the responsibility of the planet to fall on someone else's shoulders." Irvin shook his head sadly and continued, "I think it is because people seem to be in a hurry all the time with the bigger faster cars and bigger roads, people seem to want things bigger, faster and better than everyone else. People seem to just be in a great big hurry to get nowhere fast now days."

27

Irvin continued, "Now days, people do not seem to understand there is only one planet and once it is destroyed it can not be replaced." Irvin said "He remembered when he was a gosling and he and his grandfather flew South that people seemed to put more back into the environment and took less out. They respected their soil and respected the animals and valued the clean water in the streams.

"I remember when there were less people to drain the ponds and fill the streams with dirty water." Irvin continued to say, "People don't seem to stop and appreciate nature anymore. They don't see the true beauty of the trees and streams that they have in front of them. They rush by everything trying to find a new way to get things done faster and hope to make more money in the long run." Irvin continues, "People are slow to realize that the planet is everyone's responsibility, unfortunately we in the animal family cannot help the cause, we can only live with what the humans do."

"I'm just happy that there are still some places where we can spend the winter and find safety and food, but it seems to get harder every year." Irvin observed. He and Ben finished their mission by scouting the coastline of North Carolina and settled in a small town called Davis that is near the outer banks of North Carolina.

33

Ben Willis grew up in Davis, North Carolina as an avid outdoorsman. His father and grandfathers have shared their knowledge of the outdoors with him since he was a young child, teaching him the value of good stewardship of our outdoors. His interest in writing stems from his desire to start sharing his knowledge of the environment with the younger generation. The author also played football at North Carolina State University, where he is still a full time student majoring in agricultural science.

Illustrator, Mary Ann Holland, was born in Greenville, South Carolina and grew up in Greensboro, North Carolina. She graduated from East Carolina College and taught first graders in the classroom, and as a reading teacher. "Miss Mary Ann" encouraged her little ones to accept and love each other and those around them through poetry, drawing and music, often playing her guitar. "Love is something if you give it away..." was one of their favorite songs. She also encouraged their love of nature, and care of Mother Earth through conservation measures. Beach sweeps, recycling projects, and simply cleaning up after themselves were on going activities. Mary Ann has, for years, happily shared her God given talents by writing poems with illustrations for those around her. Several of her poems have been published and she has illustrated four other children's books. Mary Ann is now retired and lives in Morehead City, North Carolina, still writing poetry, playing guitar, and illustrating. She feels very blessed to have had the opportunity to illustrate this children's book for Ben Willis, reminding all of us, that each can help, and has the responsibility for the care of our planet.

I dedicate my illustrations to my son, Ben, who has always been an inspiration to me.

LaVergne, TN USA
17 November 2010
205262LV00001B

9 781452 046334